# Dr. Hill's Poet

Jeffrey Ross

Based on "Dr. Hill's Story" which appeared originally in *At the Community College: Smiles and Reflections* (Rogue Phoenix Press, 2019) by Jeffrey Ross.

**Poems included by Courtney Rene**
Seed
Butterflies
Love's Destiny

**Thomas Hardy Poems** appear courtesy Public Domain
**Walt Whitman Quotes** appear courtesy Public Domain

**Editing:** Arlo Young
**Cover Design Concepts:** Courtney Rene
**Final Cover:** Designs: by Ms. G

## Cassandra

From the Greek name Κασσάνδρα (Kassandra), derived from possibly κέκασμαι (kekasmai) meaning "to excel, to shine" and ἀνήρ (aner) meaning "man" (genitive ἀνδρός). (courtesy Behindthename.com)

## The Year's Awakening

How do you know that the pilgrim track
Along the belting zodiac
Swept by the sun in his seeming rounds
Is traced by now to the Fishes' bounds
And into the Ram, when weeks of cloud
Have wrapt the sky in a clammy shroud,
And never as yet a tinct of spring
Has shown in the Earth's apparelling;
O vespering bird, how do you know,
How do you know?
How do you know, deep underground,
Hid in your bed from sight and sound,
Without a turn in temperature,
With weather life can scarce endure,
That light has won a fraction's strength,
And day put on some moments' length,
Whereof in merest rote will come,
Weeks hence, mild airs that do not numb;
O crocus root, how do you know,
**How do you know?**

—Thomas Hardy

Do anything, but let it produce joy.

– Walt Whitman

## Ankle Deep

She stands ankle deep in our humble lake,
Wearing a one-piece suit,
Slathered in vectored oil and mystery
Those sculpted legs reflected by calm water
Esperito perfection.
Her divine silhouette demands attention: the worshipful kind
A copious focus due a sprite or naiad or goddess.
Robins and blue jays sing to her.
Butterflies perform a delicate and crowning dance
Against the tree-framed sky.
And her laughter calms the prairie breeze and shakes my heart.
Yes, I watch, joyfully empowered and free
Knowing I have finally conquered the dark tragedies of time, space, and age.

—Samuel Hill, PhD

# Prelude September 2019

Dr. Hill drove away from the small yet lovely university campus feeling weary. The late summer Nebraska air was hot and humid, but not nearly as thick and oppressive as the meeting he just left. He enjoyed his work, his teaching, his students, but the daily grind was another matter. He had been in this business so long even software upgrade training and social justice issues were starting to simmer like ancient news. Higher education seemed to be moving farther away from teaching and learning and academics. Hill wasn't sure what has happening. Things were different these days. The world was changing rapidly. But he had no dog in the fight. And he was a man of scholastic peace. This was the Friday before Labor Day weekend, and he had three days off before the fall semester began.

He would admit these days he was more interested in reading about new motorcycle engine designs than hearing about online chat rooms. Samuel Hill turned up the radio in his jeep and caught the last few bars of "Cat Scratch Fever" on a Grand Island FM Station. The song reminded him he was going to start an article questioning the significance of rock music in western culture. He wondered when rock music would decline in popularity. Probably when the last boomer passed. Or such music became politically incorrect. He didn't use his phone to play music. Nor did he own an iPod.

The 20th century jeep radio probably wouldn't support an aux cord anyway. Any notion of playlists and buying songs appeared odd to him. Reflecting, he realized he might have purchased a few LP's back in the 1970s. And maybe an 8 track or cassette tape. But not many. He wondered when free FM broadcast radio would finally be finished. Satellite fee-based radio was very popular these days. And iPhones were filled with downloaded songs. Oh well.

Prof. Hill was going through a period of change and adjustment. Just four short months ago, Samuel Hill had retired from his full-time faculty job at Copperfield Community College back in North New Mexico. His thirty-year stint of grading essays, division meetings, and holiday potlucks had finally concluded. Sure was a fast thirty years, he thought, as he turned down the gravel road to his new home. He was starting a fresh chapter in life and looking forward to his future.

Earlier, during May, he had driven his motor home (pulling his jeep along behind) to see his good friend August Nightingale in Nebraska. He ended up staying.

When he first arrived in Nebraska, in June, Doc Hill had spent about a week in Aurora, just twenty miles to the south of Lone Tree, with his RV parked out in front of Nightingale's home. For a day or two, he and the Nightingales enjoyed catching up on Copperfield and Hamilton City news. Nighty and his wife, Sarah, had each lived in Hamilton City earlier. Dr. Nightingale had worked at Copperfield for a time. Nightingale had been a policy researcher for the college, and Sarah had worked in a medical records office. Dr. Hill was amazed the couple got along so well. She had helped Nighty convalesce after he was injured in an auto accident, and they fell in love and married a year or so later. (The Nightingales' complete love story can be found in *The Auroran: Cold Front Redemption*, Rogue Phoenix Press, 2016.) They were infatuated with the area and were keen on the "healing" qualities possessed by small Midwestern towns. Hill was quite impressed Sarah and August seemed to genuinely care for each other. Their relationship did not have that "domestic" aroma or small business quality so common to stale American marriages.

A bachelor for many years, Hill had never admired or understood the marital situation. But the Nightingales were generous, pleasant people. And he learned a great deal about the local area from them. At the time, he had no idea he would soon be one of their neighbors, though a few miles away.

Now, in very early September, he lived in a small studio cabin on the banks of Pi Lake, a water-filled sandpit not far from Lone Tree and about twenty miles north of Aurora. He rented the red cabin from an attorney in Sioux City. The place had a nice porch, a pot belly stove, a loft, a kitchen, and a bathroom. Dr. Hill's motor home and jeep were kept nearby in a western movie set-like stand of trees under a large cottonwood, sheltered from the late summer sun. He was planning to live in the cabin for just one year, but he liked the place. He liked it a lot. The lake was a getaway for the attorney and his wife, but they were traveling in Europe for an extended vacation and were happy to find a tenant.

While visiting the Nightingales in Aurora, Hill read an ad in the local paper about adjunct teaching openings at University of Nebraska-Lone Tree. At about the same moment, he saw the Pi Lake cabin for rent notice. The coincidence was amazing. He had been a community college professor who had always wanted to teach at a university. And, he thought it would be Thoreau-like, almost romantic, to live in a cabin near a body of water.

Apparently, the university had a section of American Lit Survey which needed an instructor. And the attorney was anxious to find a tenant before he flew to Berlin. A couple of Skype interviews and phone calls later, both deals were consummated. When things came together, Dr. Hill was ecstatic and almost relieved. He had a cabin on the lake and a nice teaching job to keep him engaged with the academic world.

# Transition

Dr. Hill enjoyed drinking a cold Miller High Life and listening to the cattle lowing during the evenings at Pi Lake. Dusk-time birds and bats flitted about the salmon-colored sky, looking for a meal, acrobats against the greying pinks and blues. This lake residence was perfect. A constant gurgling and murmuring of the inlet stream, the wail of a suspect mountain lion late at night, the slap of beaver tails on the calm water surface: these sounds were more potent, more musical, than any symphony to the part-time professor.

This summer, while his former colleagues rode tour busses around Brussels, or hoped for sanctuary in Toronto, or wandered around Times Square in NYC enjoying the lights, he dipped his wrinkled toes into the lake and felt redeemed. The cattle, the grasshoppers, the gymnastic butterflies: none cared a hoot for politics, careers, or chatter about movies, restaurants, or coffee houses. But the whispers of cedars and poplars on a breezy day were surely the music of the spheres, the stuff of stars.

Pi Lake formed when sand was dredged out from a pit near the Platte River. The Platte, a "mile wide and an inch deep," meandered down from the Rockies and into Nebraska, finally committing itself to the Missouri River near the city of Plattsmouth. A geologist would tell you the river's sandy banks and valley were the eroded remnants of those vast mountains to the west. Hill thought, more poetically, the Platte represented a little slice of western desert cutting through the rich, black, fertile Nebraska farmland. He had even discovered a beat-up looking small prickly pear in a bluestem grass stand one morning while hiking around the lake. But cactus plants were rare here in Merrick County. Along the river bottom and tributaries and lakes, cedars, poplars, cottonwoods, and grasses were plentiful. Hill found this a magical environment, something far different than the 4500-foot elevation pinion forest he had left behind in North New Mexico

Dr. Hill had sold his 1950s era three-bedroom ranch house (with a one car carport, evaporative cooler, and a shingled roof) back in Hamilton City, North New Mexico, when he retired from CCC and left full-time teaching. Somehow, regretfully, he also sold his Ducati 750 SS sport bike. This motorcycle liquidation was most painful to him, but he had to move on, had to shed the old skin. He knew other motorbikes awaited him. Hill then bought a nice used 2005 Three Winds motor home, hitched up his 1984 jeep, and left town. He had turned into a solitary reverse snowbird heading north to retirement.

His plan had been to rent a place in Nebraska (accomplished) for a year or two and work on a book or write articles as he became used to the retired life (no movement on this front). At sixty-three, he was young yet. He had a few relatives in Arizona and North New Mexico, but he was ready to try something new. This lake residence fit the bill; however, he was initially convinced he would live in the motor home and use the cabin for a studio or office. The cabin seemed almost holy or sacred to him: a place for the arts, a place of dreams, not a catch-all for daily detritus or the smells of cooking. And he wanted to use space efficiently.

Besides, his late-model motor home had a nice bedroom at the back, an efficient kitchen, and a modern propane stove. His clothes and personal items were packaged in the storage compartments and closets. The red cabin was spacious, but the structure didn't have storage space. Dr. Hill thought about purchasing or renting a small building and having such a structure brought out here to the cabin lot. A shed would give him more storage for sure. Well, he would consider such a building later, sometime before Halloween and bad weather.

His RV also had a satellite dish and an internet link. If he hadn't committed to teaching, well, he could do without the internet. He had three battery-powered AM radios and that FM superstation in the jeep. But in reality, the professor would need email to communicate with students and his few friends back in the Southwest.

The cabin sat about twenty yards above the waterline. Some nice maple trees planted back in the 1970s by the attorney's grandfather made for a majestic shade pool. There was a pump house sitting just off to the east of the cabin. A floating boat dock stretched out about ten feet from the shore. Sometimes Dr. Hill would sit in a lawn chair on the dock and use a cane pole and bobber and worms to catch bluegills. Comfortable and calm, he would think about the book he intended to write.

Dr. Hill hoped to write a novel, a powerful literary work, during his first year of retirement. This was a daunting, a haunting task for him. His plan to begin was always on the back burner while ideas swam around in his head like a school of crappies. Oh, he had notes scattered around on pieces of paper, and character outlines on his computer, and visions dancing before him almost hourly. But beginning this project was difficult. Not because he couldn't write.

During the last ten years, Hill had written and published numerous op-eds on community college purpose and higher education in general, and "scads" of articles on teaching practices and curriculum ideas. Ho hum. Boring. He tried to publish his many poems, but to this point had no success with such endeavors. Hill had neither the gift of jangly marketing verse nor the academic MFA training to churn out those obtuse poems no one but other grad students could understand. In his more rational moments, he realized the poetry rejections had much do with his inability to successfully generate his novel. He wanted to be an artist (heart), but he seemed to be a craftsman (head).

Dr. Hill knew another community college professor who struggled with the art making complex. His friend Adam Swiss had left the college teaching world to become a musician. That didn't work out. Crazy Swiss actually had a good teaching job somewhere in the Midwest, gave it up, and currently worked as a maintenance man in a trailer park in Hamilton City and tried to promote himself as a patio singer at local restaurants and taverns. Hill had lost touch with Swiss as of late, but he remembered going to see him play at a Moonbucks once or twice.

He also remembered Swiss nervously glancing at the tip jar, which was empty. No one was paying attention to him while he croaked out sort of interesting acoustic versions of Def Leppard songs. Dr. Hill always thought Swiss was too old and too nutty to think he could make it as a musician, but whatever. His choice of songs and the performance context seemed to be at odds too. Dr. Hill remembered, suddenly, his friend Swiss had a bad reputation around Hamilton city as a ladies' man, especially with married women. Hmm.

Well, I'm not Swiss, he thought to himself. Those pretend musicians are all crazy anyway. I have a little bit of a publication track record. I just need a creative scaffold to get moving on this thing. Just some kind of hook to hang my literary hat on.

Hill liked to consider the art and craft dichotomy. Probably too much. One of his favorite authors was Edgar Allen Poe (a writer and a poet). In grad school, Dr. Hill had learned that Poe was not part of the moral tradition (Thoreau, Whittier, Emerson) of the 19th century. Rather, he was an aesthete, an artist, who sought to reunify a broken reality in most of his short stories and poems. Poe made great art out of macabre themes. This notion of unifying art and living, living an aesthetic rather than a crafted life, well, this haunted Professor Hill. Somehow, in his forthcoming novel, he wanted to work out that theme, that motif. Not the life of an artist, or of a person who enjoys looking at paintings in a gallery, but a life combining an aesthetic sensibility with morality. So far, he just couldn't figure out what to do. But he thought living in a nice idyllic setting, and also teaching a course at the university, might get him inspired. And he sure loved the beautiful lake where he lived now.

Hill enjoyed sleeping on the patio of the red cabin. The area was fully enclosed, and the small building had several large windows that could be opened for fresh air. The view of the lake was perfect from the patio. Professor Hill enjoyed mornings the best. He could watch fish jumping and birds dipping at the surface of the water before the day revved up. On some mornings, equally pleasing, the lake at sunrise was mirror smooth and untroubled.

He liked to recline on a cot, covered by a blanket or two, always wearing a pair of shorts. Sam sensed chilly fall weather might force him back into his motor home, but he thoroughly enjoyed his sleeping arrangements during the summer.

Though rural, the area wasn't always totally peaceful. Laughter from other, out-of-sight cabins rippled across the lake occasionally. Sometimes a few cattle would move down the road just outside the fenced property line. Their mooing and thrashing about would occasionally wake him just before dawn. Once or twice in July, a crop-dusting airplane scooted over the trees and headed to a nearby soybean stand or cornfield. The lake was blessed with a shoreline thick with trees. Sandy beaches were dotted by lovely wildflowers. This landscape was much different than the prairie, pasture, and farmland encompassing much of Nebraska.

Far in the distance, he could see a row of tall, white, wind turbines churning away, generating power: artifice on an otherwise perfect landscape. Times were changing, that's for sure.

# Reflections

Dr. Samuel Hill was at that age when an individual begins to reflect on significant moments and themes of his past and how certain events shaped him. He hadn't been a particularly good student in grade school or in high school, but he persevered and graduated without trouble. He was never much of an athlete, but as a kid, he enjoyed riding motocross bikes in the desert and working on two-stroke engines.

He had more or less missed out on social experiences typical to junior high and high school students. Adolescent Hill didn't go to any proms, dances, or parties. He didn't know how to behave around his high school peers. Especially around girls.

## Long Ago

I was silly, long ago.

I thought those cute girls were interested in me. Or should be.

Oh, I wasn't the best looking, not at all. I was thin and probably showed signs of inadequate nutrition as a child, or impolite behavior, or misplaced small-town narcissism. I owned two or three pairs of jeans and a shirt or two, and always looked the same: unkempt and erratic.

I didn't have any money. I rode a 1958 Triumph and could only talk about fishing or lonely motorcycle rides on cold Kansas concrete highways.

I was keen on worthless things like mysteries of the chilly Canadian north, blond furniture in 19<sup>th</sup> century stone houses, pickled beets, and the glorious smell of burning leaves on late October evenings.

I wanted desperately, while sitting on a hay bale, to hold some pretty girl's gloved hand and huddle around a bonfire with other happy couples.

Of course, the young ladies I knew I flirted with them, and tried silly games with them, and made some foolish boasts to them,

Well, they moved on to real life.

At sixteen or so, his immediate ambition was to work in a motorcycle shop, but his parents would hear nothing about such an idea. They wanted him to go to college and "make something" out of himself. So, through a strange pathway of junior college, college, two universities, and stopping out and dropping out a few times, he ended up as a community college English professor. He held a PhD in American Lit (Whitman), but most of his career had been spent teaching ENG composition courses. He had read so many essays, graded so many papers, attended so many meetings.

His dad had given him some simple advice, all those years ago, which turned out to be invaluable. "Just get a degree in something. Anything. You will be better off with a degree." So Hill, after a few starts and stops, became an English major. Reading books and writing about them seemed easy, and interesting, to the blue-collar lad. He ended up having forty-eight credit hours of English for his BA, thirty-six for his MA, and another forty-five for the doctorate. Not always as trouble free as he hoped, but he finished his formal schooling by age thirty-one. He didn't even have to borrow much money. Sam Hill enjoyed living "close to the bone." Besides, as his academic life progressed, he found he enjoyed reading poems by Roethke or novels by Updike more than going to movies, tailgate parties, or expensive restaurants. You might say he had different priorities, especially as the literature he studied began to impact his thinking and values.

Both perseverance and chance landed him on the faculty at Copperfield Community. After spending five unsteady years in college and five more in graduate school, weary Hill had been working as a daytime fertilizer salesman in Hamilton City and spending evenings as a tutor for Copperfield Community College. He began teaching part-time, a class or two each semester, and then obtained a full-time position when the college opened a store front operation in Santa Fe. That was how his "academic" life began in 1987.

Sometimes Hill wondered how his passion for Shelley and Wordsworth and Whitman got him involved in teaching ENG composition at a community college. He had always been interested in making "spiritual sense" of the natural world. Sam had found, of all the literary work he had studied to date, Walt Whitman's catalogs of animals and botanical forms and his constructs about democracy and organic divinity in *Song of Myself* to be most relevant to his own world view. His dissertation study, *Hidden Angels in Whitman's Leaves of Grass*, was mightily unrelated to teaching writing in comp classes. Ah, art and craft again. But he wasn't complaining. Maybe just surprised his career morphed into writing instruction rather than literary analysis.

Hill would admit he had always promoted good technical writing skills (punctuation, spelling, paragraphs) rather than political empowerment. In his later years at CCC, he frequently told his students his job was to help them write clearly, not further his or their political agendas. He was simply worn out on politics and the many scoundrels who ran for public office.

But recently, post community college, he had signed on to teach at the U. He felt good about the course, and Hill looked forward to reading some of his old research materials and the classic American Lit texts from the 19th and 20th century. He assumed most of the students would be sophomores and a few might even be English majors. Hill wondered, suddenly, what English majors studied today. Of course, the mystery surrounding the English major was nothing new. When he told new acquaintances he was an English professor, their usual reply or reaction was something like, "Oh, you teach Shakespeare!" Truth of the matter was, he had never taught Shakespeare, except maybe *Romeo and Juliet* or *Hamlet* in an introductory lit class. (By the way, some of those folks also said, "I guess I better watch my grammar when I talk to you!") Yes, thought Dr. Hill, the ubiquitous notions about English teachers die hard.

The English major idea muddied up art and craft, too. Novelists were artists, but there was little art in the study of transformational or structural grammar. And being able to talk about great literature had nothing to do with writing a fetching short story, at least in Dr. Hill's mind.

He found it rather odd English departments perennially thought art could be taught through creative writing programs.

Hill had always been attracted to the science of linguistics and the terse sentence parsing attributes of structural grammar. Maybe that is where he should have done his doctoral work. Nah. He loved Whitman and his munificent lists and catalogs.

# School Begins

The first day of instruction went well. UN-LT followed a four-day work week. Hill's Lit 210 class was scheduled on T-Th from 9-10:30 am. Nineteen students were enrolled in the course. UN-LT, in the rather traditionalist manner, started the regular fall semester the day after Labor Day, so his young scholars were subdued the first Tuesday morning following summer vacation. He was surprised the class mirrored a community college group in terms of demographics. All ages seemed represented.

He made the usual first day speech by talking about the textbook, attendance, learning outcomes, and the syllabus. He fired up the LED projector and showed the group how he would use the UN-LT RedBoard course management software. He admonished them to use email to contact him. Dr Hill noted that because he was an adjunct, he had no regular office hours but would be available in the UN-LT Adjunct Faculty Office for an hour after class if anybody wanted to visit with him. (After about a week of trying to visit with students in the commotion-filled "community" Adjunct Faculty Office, he told everyone he would be happy to meet with them in the Lone Tree Café for coffee or lunch. This arrangement worked out much better for everyone.)

He asked them to leave their smartphones alone during class, but also realized such advice was futile. Dr. Hill encouraged the students to introduce themselves and mention a little about their long-term plans. He paid attention to the brief autobiographical "speeches," but there was a lot of information to process quickly. Hill knew it would take a few class meetings to get to know them, but he was usually good with names by the third week or so. He provided a handout detailing information about general themes in 19<sup>th</sup> century American literature and cheerily dismissed them for the day. The professor was feeling very tired after only one hour that first morning. He was always glad to get any first day meeting out of the way. Initial course meetings just wore him out and seemed to be more tiring the last couple of semesters.

After class, Prof. Hill found his way over to the UN-LT Student Union. Inside, the Lone Tree Café had a "special": their Famous Lonely Burger, medium drink, and Corny Fries for $4.99. Wow! Such a deal! Hill planned to bring his lunch most days, but he decided to splurge on a burger. First day of school, he mused, and I deserve a treat. Hill was basically a very frugal man.

Dr. Hill didn't know anyone in the student union. Or at the university, for that matter, except for a few of his fellow adjuncts and the division chair, Dr. Farfrae. Hill ate quietly and rapidly read through a copy of the handout he had passed out earlier. As he was on the third bite of his Lonely Burger (a very tasty half-pound of beef smothered in Hundred-Island dressing on an onion bun), he sensed someone approaching and standing next to him. He wiped off his mouth and looked up.

"Hello, Professor Hill," she said directly. "My name is Cassandra. I'm in your morning lit class. Is it okay if I sit down with you for a second? I have a question about the handout you gave us."

"Oh, sure, sit down," mumbled mannered Hill, moving his backpack, fries, drink cup, and computer. He glanced at her quickly, noticing she was a trim and smiling blond lady about forty years of age with a laptop case. "How can I help you?"

She adjusted herself in the stackable dining room chair and gazed at him in a strange manner. After an awkward forty seconds or so, she spoke again. "Dr. Hill, do you remember me? Not from this morning. I mean from Hamilton City and Copperfield Community College. Like maybe ten years ago?"

Hill didn't know what to say. *What a bizarre moment* flashed through his mind. She looked vaguely familiar, but ten years was twenty semesters was 30,000 essays ago. He measured his words carefully.

"Good to see you again, Cassandra. Did I have you as a student in a comp class? You sure do look familiar to me."

"I thought you might remember me. No, I never had you for a class. Prof. Jack Frost was my English teacher. But I attended the Creative Writing Club meetings a few times. You were the sponsor. I loved your poetry."

Dr. Hill thought back to the CWC meetings at CCC, and he did recollect her. Yes. Cassandra. Charming then and charming now. And he appreciated her remarks about his poetry. He also remembered a poem he had written about his friend Frost. That professor was quite the eccentric. Last Hill heard, Doc Frost was still living in a small travel trailer just outside Hamilton City on a vacant county lot. Down by the Rio Grande River.

# Professor Frost is Rich

Dr. Frost is a funny guy.
Or odd. He never puts anything in the recycle bin.
One of his neighbors was critical.

"What the h—, said old Frost.
I'm not a consumer.
I have a flip phone, a four-cubic-foot refrigerator, and a few pairs of jeans
and t-shirts I bought at a garage sale.
I watch you Chinchillas tearing down the road in them big SUV's,
burnin' up the gas for nothing. Where are you going?
What do you know? Shop? Hah. I need a few apples, some milk, peanut
butter, corn flakes, bread, vegetables, and coffee. I can get it all in
Hamilton City.
Restaurants? Gah. The out-of-shape people come and go, come and go,
eat and spend, and two days later, cannot remember where they have
been. Hurry back to the buffet line, laddie!"

"Music? Pah.
How many !@#$% times do you need to hear Lady Gaga?
Get yourself a guitar or sax or something. How many trees does it take
to make one iPod?
I've got a Bible, Wordsworth, Blake, Stanley Fish, Contento & Ross, and
AR Ammons.

"Yep, I live out here along the road in my travel trailer, and I watch you people.

Quite entertaining. Where are you going? What do you Know?

Excuse me while I return to my bowl of cereal and *The Prelude*. Good luck to you. You need it. Bad."

Hill stopped reflecting. "Sure, I remember. Wow. Ten years. What brings you to UN-LT? Hard to believe we would meet again way out here in Nebraska! And in Lone Tree at that!"

She looked at him reservedly. "My husband, er, former husband, Robert, got transferred here in 2010 or so. I don't think you ever met him. He works for a center pivot irrigation company. Hamilton City is apparently their furthest west office. We actually lived in Aurora, out by the airport, for a few years. He became involved with a Marquette farmer's wife and left me. It was kind of messy. But the new romance didn't work out for him, or so I have heard. Maybe karma caught up to him. Sorry. Too much information for you regardless, probably. Anyway, we got divorced, sold everything, and I moved up to Lone Tree. I have my own bookkeeping business and take classes here at the college. I'm pretty much over my earlier life. I just want to move forward. I enjoy school and my job. And my doggie, Trout."

Hill had to be careful. "I am sorry to hear about your marriage, but sounds like you are back on your feet and doing well. I am glad you enrolled in our class. No doubt we share some common acquaintances in Hamilton City. Do you know if there is a creative writing club here? I am teaching just the one class and would like to learn more about the school's activities and culture.

Cassandra smiled. "Yes, the club is called Voices of Lone Tree. They have their first fall semester meeting next week. I think the agenda is posted on the LT home page. Oh, I have to go. I have Psych 203 with Dr. Alexandra coming up. Boy, he's a card! See you in class!" Hill smiled and waved as she walked away. Hill was a bit bewildered, somewhat emotional. Hill was typically an emotionally "distant" kind of guy. But this meeting with Cassandra made him feel unbalanced. Sort of un-centered (or maybe re-centered). Very odd.

# September

The month rolled by as summer turned to fall. End of September was warm and dry. The Tuesday and Thursday class ambled along comfortably. Dr. Hill followed the syllabus closely. His scholars read pieces by indigent North American people, early Spanish explorers, and the Puritans. Crazy old Hill believed in the disappearing notion of "art for art's sake," and he tried mightily to ignore contemporary issues and politics. Years ago, he had published an online op-ed about his teaching philosophy and mentioned how he worked very hard at keeping politics and personal agendas out of his classroom. Several of his readers left comments claiming such a thing was impossible. One of his detractors, a PhD from Yale, commented that Hill's claim he was not political was political in itself. Such an observation left Hill scratching his head. Well, his critics didn't know Hill. He was unlike many of his higher education colleagues.

Typically, he took his lunch on Tuesdays, and he bought a burger or chicken nuggets at the Café on Thursdays. He stopped in briefly, for just a few minutes, at two weekly writing club meetings but didn't share any of his poetry or prose. On the weekends, he fished some and gradually personalized his new living spaces. Hill noticed a woodchuck was living under the cabin and thought about finding a humane way to trap the rascal and move him further away. Things were moving along pretty smoothly, except….

Except he was thinking more and more about Cassandra. He

knew this was complicated on every level. Of course, he saw her in class. His interactions with her there were nothing out of the ordinary. She had stopped by to have lunch with him twice more. He also had lunch and coffee with several other students. Since he didn't have a private office on campus, the café became an effective place for him to meet with learners and talk about the readings and assignments.

But what conversations he did have with Cassandra in the café were strangely powerful. For example, on Thursday, the 26th, she stopped by his table in passing, again before her Psych class. Cassandra complimented him on a poem called *Joe's Girl is Big* that he had written and read at a Copperfield writing club meeting nearly twelve years earlier. (The poem basically describes an "unattractive" couple sitting on bar stools, eating cheesy fries, and loving each other, totally oblivious to snarky bystanders.)

## Joe's Girl is Big

She's got jowls and big hams for thighs...
Poor thing
Who knows where she finds those jeans?
Her little blue eyes twinkle like wing-flapping chickadees, and her laugh
is a stampede
His girl is big…
Oh, Joe hears the whispers and snickers and nasty remarks
About her size and about him and about them
But Joe will tell you.
He wouldn't trade her for a super model, and here's why:
She loves him, not in the Hollywood kind of way, she's no Bond girl.
But in real terms, real simple terms, in the way a man wants to be loved,
She loves him and is nice to him.
She is nice to him and respects him.
When they are sitting together in the Nose Guard Pub, blowing nebular

smoke rings from their Camel Lights, eating pickled eggs, and cheering
at the tele, arm and arm, two big bears on tiny stools,
Well, they are happy, my friend, and their little sudsy pint-clover moment
is the galaxy.
Time and space have no meaning for these lovebirds.
Every Friday and Saturday, you'll see them on the same two stools,
sometimes three stools, laughing and loving and putting away fish and
chips and drinking and smoking, arm in arm,
and loving each other like you can't imagine.
Joe's girl is big, and she always asks him how his day at work went, and
she wonders about his problems, and his sadness, and misgivings.
Joe isn't all that small himself.
And she doesn't complain or try to control him.
Joe's girl is big. And he loves her. And she loves him.
And they are nice to each other without script or agenda.
And what I think or what you think doesn't matter.
Joe's girl is big. Joe isn't all that small himself.


Cassandra said, "I found the poem in a notebook. I remember
thinking at the time *Joe's Girl* was very telling. Dr. Hill, your poem says
a lot about how unconditional any love should be. You seem to have an
amazing understanding of how successful relationships should
function."

Hill smiled. "Uh, well, I guess so. At my age I have seen a lot of
water under the bridge. That poem was my attempt to show how people
get together, and fall in love, on their own terms. I suppose many would
find them an unattractive pair. Joe and his girl are not glamorous in terms
of Hollywood or romance novels or whatever. But they are very happy
with each other. Joe and his girl are not 'beautiful' people. But their love
is beautiful. And more. As I read that poem now, well, I wish I would
have worked more on the aesthetic nature of their romance. Great
meaning is constructed, emotionally and intellectually, by successful

coupling. The meaning is highly compressed and contextualized, a 'microverse' rather than a universe. The poet Keats wrote, 'Beauty is truth, truth beauty—that is all Ye know on earth, and all ye need to know.'" Hill paused for a moment, realizing he was beginning to wander.

Hill scowled just a bit. "Sorry, I'm thinking out loud. I wish I could better explain how I believe love, beauty, art, and truth are related. But Joe and his girl are truthful, and loving, and that is a special kind of art. And beauty. Some sort of aesthetic unity or harmony."

She gazed at him intently. "I think you have explained your ideas quite well, Professor. Quite well."

He grinned. "I guess love is all that ultimately matters, even if a good relationship can't be explained. And cheesy fries. Don't forget the cheesy fries. Yes, very important. But I'm not a psychologist. Or a chef. Hah!"

Cassandra smiled carefully. "Dr. Hill, I probably shouldn't ask, but are you married?"

He wasn't taken back by her question. She had this "way" about her. Not artful but artistic. Talking with her seemed normal or comfortable. And her voice was musical, almost lyrical. "No. I was married in the eighties for five or six years. Didn't work out. She wanted more than I could provide. But she was rather, uh, young. So was I. Her second husband gave her a large home and a family. Good guy, really. Perhaps my diametric persona. Oh well, all the drama was several decades ago. I guess I've had a long, long, while to think about relationships and coupling. I'm at way late middle age, you know, but still perceptive. Times have changed, but human behaviors seem the same to me."

"What do you mean?" she asked, completely engaged. Dr. Hill was quick to reply. "Oh, it sure seems to me like biology and emotions always bring people together despite what is going on with technology or finances or world events. I guess it is human nature in an out-of-time or ahistorical sense. People want to couple up, and the coupling process has always fascinated me. It is so powerful, so instinctual, so irresistible. I'm completely amazed at coupling."

She sat down at his table and looked him directly in the eyes. "Do you think destiny brings people together? Fate? The Spinner of Years?"

Dr. Hill smiled broadly at her Thomas Hardy reference. "I didn't," he found himself saying. "I'm good at some kinds of perceptions, but destiny is pretty big!"

Laughing, she suddenly got up and headed to her other class. The professor stared at his hamburger and felt lighter at heart. Sam Hill was older than he wanted to be, but at that moment, he so appreciated her.

# October

Motivated by Cassandra's interest in his poetry, Hill finally stayed for a complete meeting of the writing club in early October. He meant to go only as an observer, not as a participant. Some white plastic chairs were set up in the UN-LT Poplar Room for the poets and authors, and a large folding table had jugs of iced tea and a few trays of catered finger foods and chips. He was very pleased to see someone had remembered to bring napkins and paper plates.

The club always had a little business to attend do. They wanted to publish a literary journal, or at least a semiannual collection of stories and poems, and so today when the meeting began, they discussed the mechanics of how to make such publications happen. Hill had some suggestions, but he kept silent. He thought he would send an email to the club president with his ideas. Hill just didn't want to seem intrusive.

The group typically had poetry readings to start things rolling after business was concluded. Students then read excerpts from their short stories and novels later in the meeting. The order of readings was random or volunteer. After everyone loaded a plate with hummus and chips and spring rolls, Cassandra decided to read one of her poems. It was quite good. The piece assessed butterflies with brevity and a refreshing terseness.

## Butterflies

Weak
Fragile
Can be destroyed with barely a thought and minimal force.
Strong
Fierce
Can travel on wings of dust, over hundreds of miles, in search of sanctuary.

Cassandra compressed her phrasings carefully, and she smiled pleasantly during the reading. Dr. Hill came away quite taken with her minimalist work. He especially enjoyed the inflection of her voice as she read. Struggling with his previous self-promise to be quiet, toward the end of the session, and after finishing his plate of finger food, he read, without much of fanfare, one of his unpublished poems. He introduced the work by indicating it concerned loneliness.

## The Empty Seat

I have a powerful recollection
Of an evening
Any evening
When I was twenty-three or so
Some girl I was dating, and another couple,
Wandered into a town square tavern
In a small Midwestern city
We sat down in a booth for burgers and talked about stuff
You know, unreflective material.
And I noticed three older guys,
Probably in their 50s,
Sitting at the bar

Eating pickled eggs and smoking Pall Malls

Sharing *Field and Stream* and laughing
Drinking Schlitz from the tall bottle
And I overheard them speaking
About the lives they used to live
And the beatings they took for nothing
And the divorces, failures, and disappointments
Their presence at the bar seemed archetypical to me
A scene played out in deep fat fryer smelling bar and grills
Since rural electrification. Or perhaps before.

Hardly empathetic,
I vowed I would never be like them: balding and fat, living in a travel
trailer down by the creek, or renting a room above the dress shop, or
struggling to keep a studio clean on the fifth floor of a crumbly brick
building which should be condemned.
But now I wonder. Perhaps, with even sideways glances they were
laughing at me, knowing full well the trouble remaining ahead, the false
dreams, the cultural chaos destined to coax and strangle me.

Clairvoyant, they could see the future of giddy young men who cavorted
in the Temple of Romantic Doom.

Many years later, I clearly remember one empty seat next to the rough
guy wearing green striped bibs and a seed a company cap.
And I know I have been anointed to take my place
In the smoky tavern
On the bricked street square
on the empty seat
of failure and redemption.

He didn't know what kind of reaction to expect. The crowd was polite when he finished. He heard a smattering of applause and subdued chatter from the twelve or so attendees. Somehow their quiet enthusiasm made his day.

Hill thoroughly enjoyed hearing the other students' poems—and sampling the snacks—and the professor was very happy he came to the meeting.

Days fluttered and classes continued. His two trips a week into Lone Tree were not significantly demanding. He had plenty of time to enjoy life in the cabin. Hill graded a few essay exams, prepared lecture notes, and corresponded by email with some of his former colleagues at CCC. His days away from campus were quite pleasant. Having lived at Pi Lake just over twelve weeks, he was still putting items away, finding boxes, and getting into the routine of grocery shopping and schoolwork. Some nights he stayed in the motor home and worked away on his laptop. But he was increasingly spending evenings in the red cabin, sleeping in the loft, and loving it. Happily, he also took small hikes, fished a little, and made trips into Aurora to see his friends the Nightingales. They introduced him to several of the interesting restaurants, the museum, and Susan's Book & Look Nook. He also came to know the fantastic downtown bar and grill The Greatview... Hill bonded with their cheeseburgers immediately.

# The Cabin

As it turned out, Cassandra was close friends with Sheri and Ryan, Dr. Hill's landlords. Cassandra and Sheri had known each other for several years. They had met on an online genealogy forum initially and then become "real time" friends later. She had visited the red cabin frequently in the summer when Ryan and Sheri came down from Sioux City to spend a few days. Oddly enough, Cassandra had learned from Sheri that a professor from Lone Tree had rented the place before becoming reacquainted with old Hill.

So, on the October evening when Cassie drove down the sandy road to stop by and say hi to Dr. Hill, unannounced, she did not feel awkward. Not one bit. She tapped on the outer porch screen door and smiled broadly when he came to greet her.

Seeing her through the screen before opening the door, Hill kept his composure. "Why hello, Cassandra. What a surprise. Are you looking for a place to fish or swim?" They laughed together, a warm laugh, not a nervous or forced laugh.

"Hah. No, Dr. Hill, I am friends with Sheri and Ryan, you know, your continent-hopping landlords. Sheri told me a Lone Tree professor had rented this place, and I suddenly had a hunch it could be you. Might have been too forward or something to ask you where you lived while we were on campus, so I thought I'd just take a drive out here and see how you were getting along." He was genuinely pleased to see her. "Well, Cassandra, small world. I am so glad you stopped by. I think you are more familiar with the place than I am, but let me show you around a little."

So, he took her out to see his RV and the pump house, and they stood on the floating dock for a moment and gazed at the lake in the cooling evening air. "Oh, Dr Hill, it is so beautiful out here. Sheri always said the lake was nearly perfect at dusk. She is so right!" They watched a few bats flit around and then the pair headed back to the cabin. "Cassandra, I am going into Aurora at seven o'clock for dinner at The Greatview with two of my friends. You might have met August Nightingale at CCC back in Hamilton City. We are going to have cheeseburgers and Pepsis. Any chance you would like to go? We can take my jeep." She was delighted. "Only if I can have a beer instead of a Pepsi," she said. "Oh fine," he retorted good naturedly. "I'll buy you a beer. Or two. But I also have a condition. Please call me Sam." And that's how things got started.

# Nighty Calls Sam

While grading some lit tests a day or so after The Greatview event, Dr. Hill received a call from Nightingale.

August: Don't you ever get tired of grading?

Sam: Yes. But the paper load in American lit is far less than in comp courses.

August: Sara and I sure enjoyed ourselves at The Greatview with you two. Sara thinks she met Cassandra somewhere else. Maybe at a book club meeting or on a Chamber committee. You two were pretty chummy in the booth, feeding each other French fries and singing "Radar Love" and all.

Sam, grimacing: Oh well, yes, we had a good time. She is a very interesting young lady. We were caught up in the spirit of the moment. No harm done.

August: Well, that's something I wanted to talk to you about. Look, we've been pals for decades. Do you think it is a good idea you are seeing her? She is twenty or thirty years younger than you, and she's in one of your classes. For God's sake, man, this isn't the sixties anymore. Or even the nineties! These communities are small. Everyone knows what's going on.

Sam felt his skin tighten up a little. He had thought of these potential issues too.

Sam: I know. Could be some difficulties. But we're not acting up on campus. I have to tell you I think I will just teach this one semester and give it up anyway. I'm sort of feeling beat or lost or something... or maybe out of touch. I'm enjoying this semester, but I don't know if I can fully sustain teaching any more. Tell you the truth, I do much better when she is around. Hmm. Maybe I need to return to Hamilton City.

August: Right, I know what you mean. But think of her too. I know she is a businesswoman in Lone Tree... might not look good for her if word gets out she is 'taking up with teacher.' Your life—not my business. Just wanted to get my two cents in. And we really like her. Really.

Sam: That's the problem, Nighty. I do too.

Nighty: Well, maybe it isn't a problem. I dunno. By the way, did you find it ironic The Greatview doesn't have a *view*? Hah. Probably not. You were too busy looking at Cassie!

Sam: Yes, very ironic. Hah. See you later.

## The Dream Keeps Coming Back

The Dream keeps coming back: nightly, or weekly, or monthly. Hard to say.
Yet the images and theme remain the same.
I am sitting in a red cabin
With a few pieces of furniture, a Formica table, and a warm fireplace
I am looking through a large window, framed and pure and crystal-like,
viewing a light-snow landscape sloping toward a frozen lake.
And she is sitting next to me on the couch, modest,
Womanly, and certainly fetching.
Andy Williams fountains "Moon River" in the shadows,
She is touching my hand, my face, and telling me she is happy,
Saying nice words to me in a warm room, fragrant with cinnamon, while we
Watch the snowflakes swirl with a cogent bliss that can almost be measured by

Heartbeats and breaths.
And by the wind-up clock ticking on the wall….
I do not want to leave this dream. I love these specters so.
And I hold her pretty hand and wonder at this moment and watch the swirling snow
My sonic joy evaporates with the dawn.
Then comes another red sun day.
Yet the dream keeps coming back.

# Cassandra

Cassandra was not feeling puppy love for her teacher. At forty-one, she knew the risks of relationships. She knew Hill was older, and better educated than her in the formal sense. Even so, he was a man, a person with strengths and weaknesses. She would like to know more about his past, only for instruction and resource, not for nostalgia or rescue.

Cassandra was not a victim, nor did she feel victimized. She had an Applied Science degree in Accounting from Copperfield Community College, and she did a thriving business working as a bookkeeper for several Merrick County farmers and businesses. She liked to dress in a trim and professional manner, kept a clean house, and enjoyed studying literature and participating in the Lone Tree Creative Writing Club. She kept her opinions to herself. Cassandra held no grudges. Yes, her husband had left her for another woman.

But she didn't miss him. He had never settled into marriage, even ten years into the relationship. They didn't have a family. He had a kind of focused Midwest perspective that wasn't always charming. Cassie sensed he enjoyed the town and the fields and the river bottoms, but he did not see her as a person outside of her domestic role in Lone Tree. They attended church and an occasional fish-fry together, but poor Robert loved center pivot irrigation systems more than he loved her. He just wasn't interested in her, or her well-being, most days.

She remembered writing a dark poem about how he treated her

years ago when she was sick for a day or two.

## Love's Fever

The night had been rough—you know, the fever came late and tried to finish me.

Sweaty and near delirious, with a hollow head and a pounding brain.

I called the college and left a message simple and direct. I wouldn't be in today....

I was sick. Bad.

My husband had been gone since dawn. I struggled up and made a cup of coffee.

Then the chills, a trilling drizzle down my backbone, forced me to bed.

I was shaking, nothing pleasant here, and my mind began to swirl around its problems, tossing and turning, tossing and turning, in a dizzy shell.

Do you know the loneliness of illness?

I phoned him, my significant, and croaked out my sickness.

Busy at work, he seemed bothered that I called him with this interrupting issue.

I asked, "When you come home, can you maybe bring me some soup, or medicine?"

"Well," he said, "no, probably not. I'm going to be home late—got a meeting with the Soil Service and some farmers. Just stay in bed.

You should take better care of yourself anyway."

With eyes becoming rock hard, with ears ringing and joints screaming, I hung up the phone and rolled over, trying to figure out if I meant more to him than wet cornfields and cut alfalfa.

She had a box of such poems. And she had no idea why she kept them.

True, Robert was a good provider, but she didn't need him or his money. Was his life narrow? Maybe. But that wasn't her problem then or ever. A woman of great practicality, sometimes Cassandra found it odd she wrote poems about emotional events.

Casandra was enjoying her life. She was able to work from home several days of the week at her condo, even though she kept a small office in downtown Lone Tree. She used the office for meeting with clients and keeping files, but much of her bookkeeping could be done on her laptop.

Cassie was a very independent woman who enjoyed taking care of herself. She drove a late model Kia Sportage and tried to ride her mountain bike as much as possible. She was not a feminist, but Cassie was skeptical about how women were portrayed in fifties and sixties television, especially in Westerns. Reflecting, she watched lots of classic John Wayne and Randolph Scott movies with her parents when she was little. And those black and white TV shows with a wife or lover who idolized and supported her gunfighter or cowboy boyfriend just drove her crazy. She often wondered if little boys grew up watching those westerns in the old days and then believed women were meant to cook dinner, raise large families, and look beautiful all the time in some kind of jacket-bodices with a draped and trimmed skirt, complete with ruffles and pleats.

However, well, there were also times she was lonely and very sad. Almost remorseful, although no one else knew it. Once, while walking through a park, she stopped to sit on a playground rocking horse. She rocked a little bit on the horse and was enjoying herself when a young man and woman walked by arm-in-arm, quite preoccupied with each other. She mentally juxtaposed the images, a middle-aged woman on a rocking horse and a young couple strolling together, and it was too much. She began weeping and returned home. It wasn't that Cassandra missed anybody in particular, but sometimes she felt she was missing on life events or opportunities because she didn't have someone special. Cassandra felt nagging tinges of regret as the years tumbled and slipped around here.

## Eucalyptus Moods

Her platform shoes smacked down hard on bricks.
She climbed the concrete stairs, fumbled at the front door.
And pushed through Eucalyptus moods.
She opened her condo's door and sniffed at stale perfume.
And when her dancing clothes were off,
her teeth cleaned, and her hair combed out…
She poured a silent cup of coffee and went to sleep alone.


Oh, she had great girlfriends, and a few male friends, too. She was out doing things constantly. Her classes at UN-Lone Tree had been very helpful in getting her involved outside of work and her immediate circle of friends. Recently, she had started dance lessons at the Merrick County Community Center. Cassandra was quite pleased with her part-time classes at the college, but the businesswoman had a bigger goal in mind.

She hoped to begin an online BA program in accounting or economics, and as of late, she had been looking into several programs at different universities. Cassie speculated about returning to North New Mexico, and possibly attending Hamilton State. Her experiences at Copperfield Community seemed like a long time ago. But she still had friends in Hamilton City. Time was flying. Very, very quickly now.

# Days Pass

A few mornings after her trip into Aurora with Nightingale, Cassandra awoke with a start and rolled off her bed while tangled up in a blanket. She nearly stepped on Trout, her Havanese dog. Cassie had been dreaming. More like she was awake thinking but didn't want to get up. She found her slippers with her bare feet and wandered into the bathroom and looked at herself in the mirror. The dog followed her, wagging his tail. Cassie sensed great changes in her life had arrived, apparently in an RV from North New Mexico. She began cooking breakfast while thinking about a pleasant phone conversation with Dr. Hill yesterday.

## A Good Idea

The morning had been calm.
She whispered, "You're a good idea…"
And made the smart phone hum
(over fields of harvested pleasure, golden in the flashing autumn sun)
Life is rich and full and good.
"I dream of lasting quality, he said, how best to govern future months
Our tufts of time and warm soft nights."
She saw dawn come through an eastern glass
While bacon sizzled in a blackened pan
And inscape changed to look without

Making happy more than what we are in essence
By enhancing what we are in act.
Cyclic time surely stops
To make a moment pure....

"What am I doing, Trout? I'm feeling great! Suddenly I am writing happy, positive poems and eating cheeseburgers and laughing at nothing." This is so unlike me. I am spending way too much time thinking about Hill. How can it be I keep writing these, uh, epiphany poems? I should focus on making more money, getting my bachelor's degree, getting out of here. But I just want to read my poems to him. What in the world? Am I in love with Doctor Hill? D—! I am! I am!"

**Love's Destiny**

I'm enjoying my life
Free at last from bad emotions
Lone Tree is a good place to be.
I make a decent living.
I like attending college
I love writing poetry

I enjoy wine tasting parties
Wonderful bagels at 6 am
Seasons come and seasons go
Once my holiday decorations were a mess
Now they are neatly packaged in bins
I love sleeping on chilly nights
With a blanket and Trout my dog
My home is neat and clean.
I will listen to friends complain about their husbands
Only for a time, before I change the subject.
Preferring recipes, scrapbooks, or town gossip.
My world is focused and certain.
Yet…
I have met someone who quakes my heart.
Just because of...well, it makes no sense
He reads my poems and listens
He's but a simple older man with few ambitions left
He's hinted how he loves me
I must decide how to love him back.
Love him correctly and without regret.
For though I am strong, and independent.
I cannot negate love's destiny.

# Merrick County's Newest Couple

As autumn progressed, Hill and Cassandra found ways to spend more and more time together when away from UN-LT. Like most happy couples, they did many things together: clipping coupons, playing board games, watching movies, shopping, walking, running errands. She spent most weekends at the cabin, and he managed to visit her condo for dinner and TV often. They were meshing on several levels. When they were with each other, things were good. Very good.

On Saturdays, they liked to get out into the farmland and wilds. Cassandra and Hill especially relished exploring the Platte River Valley. Sometimes she enjoyed riding her mountain bike while Hill jogged beside her. Other times they wore back packs and walked along gravel roads and pasture pathways. Some days they took driving trips through Merrick and Hall counties. They came to anticipate adventures and fun times as they began to know each other better.

One pleasant day, while motoring along in Hill's jeep toward Hordville on the W road, Sam and Cassie stopped to admire a pasture filled with drying but green sunflowers. (The field was close to the Covenant Poplars Gospel Camp.) Cassandra had a particular love for this kind of flower. Sunflowers were strong and vibrant and a powerful symbol of perseverance. Hill thought it rather odd such a field of sunflowers existed here, wedged in between two cornfields. But he, too, was taken with their beauty and majesty.

## Sunflowers

**Seed**
Nothing exciting
Black with stripes of gray and white
Rain falls and pummels the seed into the ground
Darkness follows, nothingness
But then a spark, a beat.

*Life*
New effort of growth
Wanting to reach the surface
Desperately pushing to feel the sun
Needing to reach the light
Then— a sprout emerging from dark soil.

*Green*
A tiny thread of green appears
Pushing through the soil
The stem thickens and grows tall
Dark green leaves present themselves along the stalk
Two by two, leaves grow in rows.

*Bud*
Up, up, the stalk continues rising
Then, a bud forms at the very toppy tip
Round and wide, still green in color
Slowly, so slowly the bud forms,
Grows, and expands.


*Flower*
One bright shiny day, a protective green layer opens
Sun warmth settles on the forming flower's heart
Bright orange and yellow seep into the green.
The brown and black center pushes outward

A flower is in full bloom.
*Sun*
The majestic sunflower loves her sun
She basks in light and warmth
Each day, she watches and follows the sun's slow sky progress
As darkness falls, the flower awaits day's return
Day after day, the flower follows the sun's path.
*Death*
All too soon, bright yellow petals grow wilted and fade
Falling and floating to the ground one by one
The brown and black center is all remaining from the sunflower's vigil
Frost and cold arrive
What is left of the summer sunflower droops—and is no more.
**Possibilities**
Black and grey matter falls from her center
Small flecks spill to the ground haphazardly
On the chilled soil they wait
All that endures from the once beautiful flower
This is not the end, as…
*Seeds*

# Dr. Dolph Farfrae

The Language and Lit Department at Lone Tree had division meetings about once a month. Dr. Hill, as an adjunct, was not required to attend. But he always made an appearance. After the October departmental meeting, the division chair, young and handsome Dr. Dolph Farfrae, asked Dr. Hill if he could spare a few minutes to visit.

Dr. Hill: Of course, Dr. Farfrae. Would you like to meet in your office?

Dr. Farfrae: Sam, let's get a cup of Moonbucks over at the café... just wanted to visit with you a minute or two. Just catch up, see how your semester is going.

Dr. Hill paid for the two medium Moonbucks coffees and wandered over to the table where the division chair was seated in a rumpled fashion. Farfrae seemed fidgety, uncomfortable, tense. He looked grumpy.

Dr. Hill: Here you go, Dolph. Stark's Place, no cream or sugar.

Dr. Farfrae: Thanks, Sam, I relish this Stark's Place coffee. It's a little pricey, but it sure is good for teaching in the evening. Keeps me wide awake. Sometimes too late, though... Then I can't sleep. Hmm. Ahh. Hmm. Well, I'll get right to the point. I've heard a little, er, gossip, around the department that you have, uh, been seen off campus with, uh, one of your female students.

Dr. Hill: Oh. Well. I cannot deny I have shared a hamburger or two with her. I'm sure you are referring to Cassandra. She is friends with my landlords. I assure you nothing in our private lives has any effect on her status as a student at Lone Tree.

Dr. Farfrae: Yes, well, I've also been advised from students and staff you frequently have lunch with her on campus.

Dr. Hill: Why yes, Dolph, that is also correct. But I have had lunch with several other of my students—and coffee meetings also. As you know, we adjuncts do not have private offices here. The café and the patio are handy and pleasant places to meet. Take note I am currently having coffee with you on campus. And I have been seen with you off campus as well.

(As he said this, Hill recognized his logic was off. Way off. Oops.)

Dr. Farfrae: I appreciate your perspective, Sam, but maybe drinking in public with her at The Greatview down in Aurora is a bit, well, inappropriate. And you were seen coming out of the condominium complex where she lives.

Dr. Hill: Yes, Dolph, you are probably right. But she is nearly forty years old and a successful businesswoman. I'm sixty-three and actually retired. Geez Dolph, am I under official surveillance? Do you truthfully think I am damaging the university's reputation by sharing hamburgers with a grown woman on a Friday night?

Dr. Farfrae: Sam, you have to be careful in this environment. We all do. You are an adjunct, and we appreciate your willingness to teach for us, but do consider how it might look to the community at large. Consider your professional status.

Dr. Hill: Ok, Dolph, I appreciate your concern. I understand your position as well as Chair. I enjoy being with her. I gather it isn't appropriate.

Then the Chair's phone burst into a Lady Gaga melody.

Dr. Farfrae: Oh... it's my wife. I've got to take this call. Thanks for the coffee, Dr. Hill.

He left the café and wandered outside, grimacing while he listened on the phone to his spouse. "Honey, that's not entirely accurate. I was at a strategic plan rewrite meeting until..." was the last thing Hill heard.

# Germany Calling

Sheri: Hi Cass... can you hear me?

Cassandra: Yes! You are very clear. Hi Sheri! Where are you?

Sheri: I'm wandering through a little German town called Kalt Wasserdoktor. Ryan and his cousin, Jeff (from Arizona who came along with us at the last moment), are at the Wasserdoktor Pub having lunch. Hah! Jeff is quite a drinker. So, I thought I'd give you a call. How's school?

Cassandra: Oh, good. I've been busy with classes. We've had good weather here this fall so no trouble getting to campus. Work is busy... quarterly taxes are due for some of my clients.

Sheri: Did you ever drive out to the cabin to meet our tenant?

Cassandra: Why, yes, I did. What a coincidence. He is one of my teachers. We have hit it off amazingly well.

Sheri: What does that mean?

Cassandra: Oh well, we've had lunch together a few times, met for coffee, that kind of thing. He is quite the poet and encourages my own writing. We even went down to The Greatview one night to meet some friends of his, the Nightingales, and ate cheeseburgers.

Sheri: (Detecting something in Cassandra's voice) Oh, very interesting. Ryan and I were introduced to the Nightingales a while back at a Husker Football Fundraiser in Grand Island. A double date with the Nightingales. Hmm. We thought Prof. Hill was a really nice guy. Quite a bit older than you, if I remember correctly. A little odd, but pleasant.

Seemed distracted easily by birds and insects.

Cassandra: Well, yes, you are right. But I am attracted to him in a rather strange way. He is very calm and confident. I just enjoy spending time with him. I don't know if eating a meal together means dating... but whatever. We like to talk about art and landscapes.

Sheri: Good for you, good for you. (Not fully meaning it.) I imagine it's time for you to get out a little since things have moved on from Robert. Maybe a harmless older guy is good, but I don't know if you should be going out with your instructor. It'll get around the square in Aurora in no time. Hmm. I was hoping to introduce you to one of Ryan's doctor friends. He's a recently divorced dermatologist, doing quite well. I think he graduated from Creighton. He enjoys traveling, hiking, and mountain biking. Maybe when we get back, I'll... Oh, I've gotta go. I see Ryan and Jeff coming down the street. Ryan is helping Jeff walk. Hah! Good talking to you, sweetie. Bye!

Cassandra: Bye Sheri. Talk to you soon!

Cassandra put down her phone and reflected. Sheri was one of her best friends. And always would be. But there was something in that phone call, in Sheri's tone of voice, Cassie just didn't like. It was sort of judgmental, or critical. "And I don't want to meet any dermatologist," she said out loud to herself. Why in the world should such a thing bother her?

# Office Hours

Dr. Hill had many beneficial after class meetings with his students at the Lone Tree Café that fall. He enjoyed visiting about American literary greats over a cup of coffee or a hamburger. Funny, he thought to himself one day while discussing Anne Hutchinson with a group of students over lunch, these writers are much more interesting with a soda and fries. On a few occasions, some Creative Writing club students stopped by to share their poems or stories. He suspected there could come a time when pollution or a pandemic might wreck face-to-face education forever, but he was very happy with "vintage" or traditional human encounters. Sometimes Cassie stopped by to sit in with a group. Occasionally they met privately out on the patio. Especially on those pleasant, dry October afternoons when the sky and sun were perfect.

Dr. Hill was changing intellectually. He was recently viewing literary figures like Whittier and Poe more as real people, not merely anthologized authors who had contributed to the canon. The professor wanted his students to read and assess literature on their own and ask their own questions, rather than expect him to tell them what to think. He found informal get togethers more productive, in terms of learning, than traditional in class instruction. One evening, while enjoying a cold drink by the lake, he wondered if it would be appropriate during class time to have his students read any of their own poetry. They *are* Americans, he mused. And the class is American Lit.

# Detached

Then, perhaps surprisingly, as the early fall days rolled by and Halloween loomed on the horizon, Hill was feeling increasingly detached or restless. He had a sense of monachopsis—the subtle but persistent feeling of being out of place.

His meeting with Farfrae and the talk about "impropriety" didn't bother him too much. Gossip occurred everywhere. He embraced his teaching life most days. Doc Hill enjoyed his class and working with his pupils. The university students seemed more focused at times than his previous community college classes, but not that much.

Anyway, something obscure was bothering him. He was suddenly feeling lonely, or tired, or out-of-touch. Very odd. He found himself turning down faculty social gatherings because he didn't want to go by himself.

## Friday Night Lights

Some other instructors and I would sit on the Moonbucks patio
And gaze treeward.
I was becoming foggy and spacious
Seeing them and their wives happy together.
Salary schedules and gossip were tossed about.
Software packages criticized; administrators lampooned.
(My part-time status freed me from most concerns but not from being

lonely.)

Another Friday night anticipating other Friday nights and better times ahead…

Prof. Farfrae shouted…. "Look! A shooting star! Is that an omen, or just a streak of bright? Will the crops fail? Will hearts break?" The group cackled with literary delight.

I flip a mental switch and consider sunflowers and butterflies…

Somehow the moment isn't right.


At times, Sam Hill was beginning to consider himself as an antique bachelor, and he didn't appreciate the construct. People didn't treat him differently because of his age. In fact, he was very respected at the university and among his local acquaintances. But he was sensing they labelled him as a funny old guy living out in the woods.

Maybe he was feeling his age. Didn't seem possible he was already in his sixties. He walked or jogged every day and worked out with some gallon jugs filled with lake water (curls and shrugs). He didn't take any maintenance medication, and he was only slightly overweight. Hill had no interest in shuffleboard or automated foot massagers. He sure missed his Ducati, and almost bought a black 2009 Kawasaki KLX 250 Supermoto advertised for sale in Hordville. (Yes, he should have bought that motorcycle. Hill just didn't want to leave it out in the rain and snow here at the cabin.)

No, it wasn't age. The mood was something more like a sense of loss or need. Things seemed to be slipping away from him.

However, Dr. Hill did not feel ambiguous or old when he was sharing a Moonbucks coffee with Cassandra or reading her poems. Shifting mental gears, he wondered if Cassandra would go riding with him on a motorcycle. Perhaps sadly, he could count on one hand the number of times any woman had ridden with him. But no. He realized it didn't ultimately matter if she shared his interest in two lane highways and degreasing engines. She had so many merits, so many strengths. Why should he care what anyone else thought? She made him very happy. Indeed.

## Bright Life

Captured by a flurried feeling
Reflecting her palm touched his
And brushing a strand of blond hair from his cardigan
He realized this splash of life polished him
And made him smile spontaneously
And cushioned every aching thought
This Bright Life spark of dreams made real
He absorbs and canonizes the moments past...
She was captain of his eyes, forever.

During one of his walks, Hill looked down at the lake from atop a sandy berm. Through evening mists and the starry dusk, he rubbed together chilly hands in the failing light. He desperately needed the cabin's light and warmth. And he longed to see Cassandra often. And see her smile and hear her voice.

"Very odd," Dr. Hill murmured to himself. He hadn't thought much about beginning his novel lately. He was becoming more interested in Cassandra's poetry. He recognized this amazing connection with her. Both of them wrote poetry, good or bad, that worked out emotional issues. Each poem was a personal trope, or figure of speech, for what was going on in life. He asked himself, what was it about Cassandra that was captivating him? The woman or her poetry? Oh, she was not Denise Levertov or Sylvia Plath. Cassandra's poetry had simple and direct messaging. She reflected on her life's events and then found a way to construct meaning on paper. Incredible.

And he thought back to her Thomas Hardy reference. Just wonderful. Hardy was a famous novelist who had longed to be recognized first for his poems. Hill had taken a Thomas Hardy seminar many years ago as a grad student at the University Nebraska. One of the best courses ever. Dr. Wright, who taught the class, was a great professor. A true Hardy scholar.

He sensed in many ways Cassandra was more "immune" to community commentary, or social norms, than he was. Not completely asocial, he had always been sensitive to outer expectations about "appropriate behavior." He considered her poetry writing might be a psychological mechanism for confronting social awareness. He shook his head. "Hill, sometimes having a doctorate doesn't pay. You think too much!" But he was changing, taking a new pathway, and there was no return for Sam Hill.

## Funny Black Magic

We are conversing on a patio
At Lone Tree, late October, nearing evening. Students, laughing and smelling like burning leaves and cornfields, come and go.
A lovely day, just a breeze, clearly meant for plen-air painting
I rambled in enthusiastically [wishing for a script]
She waved to me from a table.
She had been writing poetry and was famished.
Her salad was suitable. I worked my way through an LT Burger [the smiling server told me, "You should try The Vegan Delite next time."]
Grasping at this moment, safe on a ninety-minute island, knowing no one recognized me for the desperate
lonely-ethos half shell hombre I might become... I listened to her speak and felt a tender happiness emerging....
Like the others, she is careful with me and sees the odd and legion stress and crises fault lines crossing my face.
[Most folks have been walking around me tenderly as of late. Perhaps they see me drifting out and away, and yet they are secretly glad to see

me go]

She asks, "Well, what would you like to be doing? Where would you like to be?" And I cannot tell the truth—it is too easy, too clear, and would shatter the universe like an unkempt string theory disaster. "Maybe you should exercise more... get out and move around."

The *dialectic* of love, my friend, has no outcome.

And Hegel has no answer for the quiet patio, and gentle talk, and the calming effects

Of a worshipful autumnal afternoon, when maple trees make hymns in the bright sunlight

And the music struggles within my heart.

# November

On a very warm November afternoon, Cassandra came out to the lake to visit with Hill. She brought along a box of runzas (a kind of hamburger roll) and loaded fries. The afternoon temperature was nearly seventy-seven degrees. A cold front was approaching and pushing warm air ahead of it. Snow was forecast in twelve hours, but the day felt like late summer. Hill had placed a card table and two folding chairs out on the floating dock. After greeting her, he went back inside to rummage around for two bottles of beer. When he came out, he didn't see her at first.

She had taken off her long sleeve shirt and shorts. Cassandra was wearing a swimsuit and standing in the water near the place where the stream entered the lake. She stood just behind some cattails, and she was paying attention to a mid-size turtle who was trying to swim against the current, up the stream and out of the lake.

Hill sat down on one of the folding chairs and watched her. He noticed a tattoo of a butterfly (partially obscured by the swimsuit) on her shoulder. Wow. She was beautiful but so much more. Her face held a kind of Whitmanesque divinity for sure. She was teaching, and reaching, him by being. And they were one-ing, becoming one, rapidly, with a loving, unstoppable momentum.

Somehow, from his frame of reference, her physical beauty complimented, or complemented, her intellect and persona. Oh, she was a looker, for sure, but he could honestly say to himself he was attracted to her because of her total self-presentation. What's that tired cliché: "Beauty is more than skin deep"? Hmm. In this case her beauty emanated from her core being or illuminated her core being. He had experienced nothing like this... or read anything to match his recent interactions with her. Why had the novelists and poets missed this characteristic, this process?

## Sharing A Blanket

After dusk, when the chilled November air fell around them...
Her lips found his....
And their potent cosmic dance began.
Love's sweetness overcame them swiftly.
Two people
embracing in the moonlight
Hearing just their beating hearts,
A harmonic cadence...
And the stream's gentle pulse.
Yes, she gave her love to him.... without a monologue or explanation.
And he saw eternity in her perfect eyes, and they left the past behind....
And that night, when the early winter tumbled and careened through the cedars
And left dancing snow sleeping on the lake banks
The couple shared a blanket, and read poems aloud, and loved through the chilly night.
The next morning found them drinking coffee and cuddled.
A future secured…

# Global Snow Melt

A few days after the light snowfall, Hill was at his café office. He was reading two popular Whitman poems ("When Lilacs Last in the Courtyard Bloomed" and "The Locomotive") and doing a little prep work for his next lit class. He felt fresh, youthful, invigorated. As he was taking notes, he heard footsteps. He looked up to see Lauren Sego. He wasn't surprised to see her. She was one of his students, but she had never come to visit him after class before. She was quite interesting. A graduate of a university in California, Lauren was working at a Lone Tree live music night club as the lighting director. Hill knew her parents lived nearby, something about in an apartment above an airplane hangar, and she was more or less taking some time away from the busy LA music scene and international touring. Lauren was quite athletic and an avid rock climber. Earlier in the semester, she told him she wanted to take a class to meet people and stay "sharp." She was also an Emily Dickinson fan. Lauren was carrying a Moonbucks coffee and an iPad.

Lauren: Hi Dr. Hill.

Hill: Hi Lauren. Good to see you. I'd buy you a coffee, but it looks like you already have one.

Lauren: Oh, thanks. That's very nice. Look, Dr. Hill, I, uh need to visit with you about something not exactly related to class but sort of related to class.

Hill: Oh. I see. What is it? How can I help you?

Lauren: Well, it's uh, kind of awkward and I guess sort of gossipy. I personally don't care, but you know, I, uh, need to tell you or ask you about something.

Suddenly telepathic, the professor knew what was coming.

Hill: Sure, go ahead, Lauren.

Lauren: Well, it's something like this. A few of the younger students in class, you know, the teenagers, wanted me to see if I could find out about what's going on with you and Cassie... er, Cassandra. You spend a lot of time with her, and people have seen you with her off campus, too.

Hill: I see. Well, you have to remember she is a little older than most of you. I don't actually see a problem in this. We are, ah, friends, and enjoy coffee and an occasional lunch together. In class I treat her just like all of you... with kindness and respect.

Lauren: Sure, I understand. They just wanted me to ask you, that's all. Oh, did you know my parents have a cabin up there at Pi Lake? I saw you and Cassie over at Ryan's cabin last weekend... you know that strangely warm afternoon. She was standing in the water. I waved at you, but I was a long way from your dock and you probably didn't see me. Or you were busy. Well, I've gotta go. See you in class, Dr. Hill.

She smiled pleasantly and ambled off.

Hill: Bye Lauren. Sorry I didn't see you at the lake. Thanks, and see you Thursday.

The professor shut his book and collected his belongings. *Great,* he thought to himself.

# Leaving

She finished her hot chocolate and gazed into the firepit. The weather had changed. This had been a very cool afternoon at the lake. Most of the birds and animals were silent or gone for the season. "Sam, how would you feel about, uh, leaving?" He was watching a beaver push a limb across the water. "What do you mean? For the afternoon?" "No," she said, "I mean like forever. At least for quite a while. Couldn't we get in your RV and take off, maybe head south for the winter like geese? As long as we have the internet, I can keep my business going, especially for a short time. I think I might start on an online degree too. Remote learning is becoming more popular all the time. We could even go back to Hamilton City eventually."

He smiled at the suggestion and mulled over the idea. The semester ended just after Thanksgiving weekend, which came early this year. "Why do you want to go, Cassandra?" He knew before she answered, but he wanted to hear it.

Cassie said with vigor, "I don't know, Sam, I would just like to get away from here for a while. We both know people around town are talking about us, and I suspect you've heard something around the college. It seems petty to me, but the talk is rather wearing. Even my closest friends are sort of, er, catty about us, because of the age difference and our other relationship at the college.

"I am not going to stop loving you because you are older than I am, or because we met in your classroom, or because we read poetry together. I don't think we can change the town, so let's go someplace different. I know you like teaching at Lone Tree, and you think this is a great place to live. Surely, Sheri and Ryan will understand if you leave early."

Hill's thoughts immediately turned to the lease. He didn't want any trouble with his landlords. "Well, I have prepaid for the year's lease. It was only $2500. That's not an issue. I think they were hoping to have someone around to keep an eye on the place. But that part would probably be okay. And I have to admit, I enjoy teaching, but I don't have to do it, especially if it is causing you, or causing us, some discomfort. Hmm. I've enjoyed living here. Back when it was warmer, I could sit out under the maple trees and grade papers and listen to the birds. Fun. We've had some great afternoons swimming and wading in the shadows. Summer lasted longer than usual. And the fall colors are wonderful. But since I've come to know you, well, I guess I see things a little differently."

For a time, they became silent, more or less lost in thought. Cassandra wondered if she sounded too pushy, or if she was the catty one, or if the whole thing was crazy. But it wasn't.

# Time and Space

I will love you Dr. Hill,
Breathing cold air
And moving through time and space.
You will make me smile
With or without whiskers on your face…
Touch my cheek, kiss my lips... do the rest
As long as you are with me, who needs a house or a place?
I want you.

Hill drifted off into a reverie about their relationship, and he began to grasp the meaning they were making with their coupling. The art manifested by their connection, if you will, was far more important to him than hearing fish splash on the lake. All of his foreboding loneliness vanished when she was near. All of it. They were both so overcome by love, sweet love, that what the townspeople thought, or the lease said, or their friends said, well…. But somehow all of the noise mattered and was troubling. Interfering. He sensed the Puritan consciousness was still strong in American society, no matter what year it was or what pop culture and social media promoted.

"Cassandra, I own some property back in Hamilton City. I have a garage I once utilized as a workshop on a quarter acre lot. I use the building mostly for storage now, and there is room for your car in there. What do you say, if we decide to leave for sure, I drive the RV and pull the jeep and you can drive your Kia? Then we can park the jeep on the lot, put your Kia in the garage, and head down south for the winter. We can leave some stuff in the building to make more space in our RV. Maybe we could dive down to Arizona for the winter and then return to Hamilton City in the spring. Just a thought."

Cassandra told Hill she liked his plan in general. After brewing a K Cup or two, they talked about the events of the day, and then she went home to get some rest.

Hill was reflective after she left. This turn of events the last two months or so surprised him, but he willingly embraced the situation. If she wanted to leave at semester's end, he would go. He found it strange, but not unnatural, that his love for her had displaced so many of his other feelings, attitudes, and behaviors.

However, he wasn't sure he wanted to be a vagabond. He wanted a home base, a place to keep a motorcycle or quad or trail bike. But he wanted her, too. And he wanted her to be happy. He knew of many couples who sold all their possessions and then travelled the country in a motor home. Such an experience seemed quite romantic to him, quite adventurous. He understood Cassandra could easily maintain most of her bookkeeping business as long as she had phone and internet service. And she could work on her BA degree online. He realized he might finally be able to start on his long-ignored novel. They would have a chance to head out of the winter snow, that's for sure. He thought he might like to voyage west, further west, to Arizona or Southern California.

But he did have some dreams persisting about building a geodesic dome or shipping container house next to the garage in North New Mexico. Hmm, he thought. I can defer my dreams. I don't have to forget them.

Hill was warming up to the idea of leaving Lone Tree. He did not like being judged by the town because of Cassandra. Funny, he thought. Nightingale and Sara vehemently believed they were healed by a small and loving community. Cassie and I have been mildly castigated. He knew the comparison did not work logically, but there was some validity to his feeling.

## Drying Time

Following a warm season
I find a plot macabre.
The prairie grass is tired, the vegetables dried.
The snow brings no hope in this weary place.
The harvest is past, hearts harden.
Halloween is put away for another year.
And my friends plan Thanksgiving without me.
I write poems for the poet I love.
While the ones I loved ignore me.

# Semester's End

And so it came to pass, the semester ended. Cassie and Sam spent Thanksgiving weekend together preparing, both formally and informally, for their departure. Hill sent an email to Dr. Farfrae advising him he would not be returning for the winter interim or spring semester. No response. His teaching tenure at UN-Lone Tree was over. Cassie contacted her clients and informed them she was closing her office and would be available to provide them bookkeeping services online only beginning December 1.

They drove into Aurora on the Saturday after Thanksgiving to have the RV checked out and fueled, and then Cassie and Sam spent a quiet evening with the Nightingales watching football and saying their goodbyes. The Nightingales saw Sam and Cassie's trip as temporary. August hinted it might be a good way for the new couple to focus on their relationship. The evening was pleasant. They topped it off by walking down to The Greatview and eating fried chicken.

Cassie put many of her belongings in storage (perhaps a sign she was returning?) and packed a few essentials for the RV road trip. She was careful to take her mountain bike for future exercise and exploration rides out west. On Sunday, they loaded up the RV and straightened up the cabin. The final exam for Hill's class was the following Tuesday. Cassie's other final was on Wednesday. They spent Thursday taking care of random loose odds and ends, and then headed out of the Lone Tree area on Friday. Weather was good, but the once-colorful trees were quickly losing leaves.

Hill drove the Three Winds with the jeep towed behind, and Cassie followed in her SUV. While he was alone, he was not lonely. Not a bit. Cassie wrote one poem while they were stopped in eastern Colorado.

## Spinnakers

Stopping off for a bite to eat
We noticed tumbleweeds spinnaker across
An open lot
And vanish into the high desert.
I can't help but feel a little dizzy here
Watching the season pillow into frenzied harshness,
then grunt and groan like chilled wildflowers.
There are many nights when frigid air turns plastic
And has a cutting edge so sharp
Even ideas seem to freeze.
Some days never seem to end.
They turn to grey then light again
And the sun stays a dull pink circle.

I have left the world I knew so long.
And feel much better. I do not see ghosts or hear voices.

I sense angels around me now…

I have the open road and Sam, a good man who listens more than he talks… who loves me in the right ways.

I cannot reveal our love secrets.

I cannot share the nighttime melodies we create.

Do we have concerns? Of course. Do we have bad days? Certainly.

But he is constant, true, and loving… and our time together is a poem, a novel, the union of all holy earthly things—a tapestry of joy and meaning…

And I love him. I love him.

# Hill Ruminates

The tight knit caravan headed down two-lane highways to North New Mexico. The one-day trip to Hamilton City would prove to be mostly uneventful. Dr. Hill kept an eye in the mirror to monitor Cassandra's progress. She was fine. He noticed she was talking on her phone a lot. He reflected people are rarely separated by time and space in the 21$^{st}$ century. Sometimes when he looked, he would see Trout sticking his head out the front passenger side window, even in forty-eight-degree air.

Always processing meaning, Sam was thinking about his new life. He had gone to Nebraska to be healed, or at least refreshed, and he was heading back home with entirely new circumstances. He had left his nice transcendental lifestyle, complete with a pond and natural symbolism, and abruptly embraced a Poe-like fascination with art forms. Especially poetry. Sort of bizarre!

He continued to try and figure out, at times, what went wrong in Lone Tree. He was quite able to compartmentalize portions of his life. To him, school was school, and his private time was his own. (Cassie earned a B in the lit class. She didn't do so well on a couple of the essay exams. Hill had simply added up her points. She told him, pointedly, Dr. Alexandra had given her an A.)

Perhaps all of the occurrences leading to Lone Tree, and the recent events in Lone Tree, were meant to happen.

Hill was completely even-tempered. He didn't altogether mind the good-natured barbs he received from his friends and colleagues about Cassie. But it became too much. Some other adjunct made a crass reference to Nabokov's *Lolita*, and that was enough. (Briefly, *Lolita* is the story of a literature professor's obsession with a twelve-year-old).

Sam Hill had loved the lake and the cabin, and all the natural world had to offer in Nebraska. Should he have become involved with Cassandra? Well, he did. Was it unethical? Not in his view. So why was it a problem? He knew the answer. It was obvious. The typical or traditional projection of morality by the community was far more powerful than art or love. He had no guilt and no bad feelings toward a soul in Lone Tree, but he wasn't going to wear a Scarlet L(ove)... and neither was Cassandra. He was thinking again about writing his novel, and he suddenly realized, near Fort Morgan, Colorado, he had all the material he needed. And it had taken a poet, a special poet, to make him understand his purpose and direction.

## In Moments

I have lived a life of introspection and review.
Assessing the past and planning the future.
Evaluating birdsongs and cricket chirps.
Always working on discrete elements.
What happened? What will come?

And she has taught me how to live
in time, in life, right now.
And the highway is my friend today.
And the touch of her hand is interstellar,
Bringing joy and loving shelter.
Cassandra, most excellent, a waking dream
Embracing life in moments....

# Butterfly Clouds

Cassie enjoyed her trip from Lone Tree to Hamilton City. Trout loved riding in a car. He spent most of his time sleeping, but once in a while he barked at other dogs he saw along the street or in other vehicles on the road. The drive took them through Nebraska, a little bit of Kansas, eastern Colorado, and then into North New Mexico. Several coordinated stops were made so she and Hill could get lunch, gas up, stretch, or take Trout out for a walk. She was on her cell phone most of the time, saying goodbye to people, and reassuring Sheri everything was going to be okay. She told her friend she was safe, and she could easily return if things didn't work out so well with Hill. But Cassie's heart knew there would be no problem with Hill. Ever.

She did receive one rather strange, totally unexpected phone call. Cassie had attended The First Order of the Prophetic Dispensation Church in Hordville a time or two, at least enough that the church had her name and her phone number. She actually took Hill to the church's 6:00 AM services one Sunday just before Halloween. She remembered they kayaked on the Platte later that morning. The call was from David F. Haymaker, Senior Pastor.

Cassie (not recognizing the number): Hello.

Pastor Haymaker: Yes, hello. Is this Cassandra? This is Pastor Dave from The First Order Church in Hordville. Do you have a few minutes?

Cassie: Yes, Pastor, I do. I am driving but I am on a nearly vacant highway. I can certainly visit with you.

Pastor Haymaker: Oh, good, good. This won't take long. As you know, our church enjoys having visitors and welcomes everyone from the local community. We are striving to do the Lord's work and try our best to be good Christians.

Cassie: Yes, Pastor, I have been to your church a few times. You are an excellent mandolin player.

Pastor Haymaker: Oh... thank you. Yes, yes. Well, uh, two ladies in the congregation have brought it to my attention, uh, you, uh, have been seen with your professor from the, uh, from the college, on numerous occasions, in drinking establishments. It is not my place, or theirs, to judge your behavior. The Lord Almighty will be your final judge, of course, but ah, we're not sure if our church is the best fit for you and Dr. Hull. We, uh, try, uh, to model more, uh, appropriate behavior. I myself know we are all steeped in sin, hopelessly fallen, but I do my best to show my sincere and honest concern for all who follow the Prophets. Yass. But the congregation, ah, well, you know, the church, ah, has a certain fascination with the Ten Commandments and the Old Testament, and, uh, well...

Cassie: Oh yes, I see. Yes. His name is actually Dr. Hill. Well, I appreciate your concern for our spiritual well-being. I must report I am returning to Hamilton City in North New Mexico, so you won't have to provide me with any spiritual counseling henceforth. Good day, Pastor Haymaker. Please take my name off your calling list. Thank you. (Click.)

Hah. Well, she thought, I might have burned that bridge. The nerve. I wonder if I'll ever see Pastor Haymaker again. Or any of them? Boy, it feels good to be on the road!

At this juncture, she still sensed this journey might be an extended winter vacation, a chance to visit warmer states, some kind of liberation and distancing from bad vibes. Maybe even a chance to enjoy Christmas in Mexico. Cassie was becoming very confident, more buoyant, as the miles rolled along, and she put Lone Tree behind her. (Ah, but some small inner prophetic voice, some jester, was whispering they might not be going back any time soon.) She was happy, Trout was happy, and Dr. Hill was happy.

Just before the sunset that afternoon (this was early December), Cassandra noticed some beautiful grey and pink clouds which resembled dancing butterflies. She called Hill, and he acknowledged the sighting. "Most beautiful," she whispered to Trout. "Just lovely. This must be my fate. But how do I know? How do I know?"

# Hamilton City

All three arrived safely in Hamilton City. They eventually parked her car in Hill's building, and Sam unpacked and then reloaded a few items in the RV. (Cassie noticed, with some degree of wonder, that Hill's facility was painted red.) His garage had sleeping quarters and a bathroom, but they decided to spend the night at the Hamilton Motor Motel in reasonable comfort. They actually ended up staying at the motel for three nights. (Trout found the bed comforter most enticing.) The lovers took a few days to visit acquaintances in Hamilton City. Cassie had left the town nearly ten years ago, but there were a few folks she wanted to contact.

The brief visit completed a bit of a loop, a past historical cycle. This was the last port of the old world, neither good nor bad, but receding rapidly from their consciousness.

On a misty mid-December morning, destiny's couple stopped to buy a couple of Moonbucks coffees and then headed down the highway toward Santa Fe. They would motor across New Mexico and Arizona, and perhaps visit San Diego or Algodones, Mexico for Christmas. Neither looked in the rear-view mirror. Trout might have.

## Couple on the Sun 2023

Tennessee Williams knew
no shadows linger on the sun

And now you know this, too
But the sun shines anyway
And the sun is bright and loving….

...


Today, they live together in an older Yuma motel
A simple two room palace smelling like ash trays, stale coffee, and enameled paint.
Three decades ago, he might have looked like a young TS Elliot.
She is yet a beauty, hardened some, and her tattoos have lost that etched and sexy look [But ach! she turns heads... and has a way any male (or female) might recognize]
Yes, they cut majestic figures together... literary but anachronistic.
Sometime, not long ago, they left public lives
(Together)
And drove their RV to this town, and thought they'd stay a day or two, walking along hand in hand, neither excited nor dismayed.

Eventually some time went by, and
they waited see if anyone was angry or perplexed.
They never heard a thing from the old world, and now, in autumnal time, live and love in a motel room.
She does her work on a laptop….
He reads and writes and watches her keenly….
He is working on his third novel,
Focused on art and life.
Bathed in golden and mote-filled sunlight every summer morning—
Refreshed by chilling desert air during pink sky winters…
And they wander hand-in-hand to the Red Caboose diner for most meals
Wearing appropriate face masks (emblazoned with golden butterfly imagery)
Coupling down cracked and tarry concrete sidewalks and considering

destiny
Writing poems, reading books, and loving.
...


He listens to the world on a 9-volt AM radio.
She reads coupon books left behind, naps in the motel lobby,
And paints her nails and adjusts earrings each morning ...
He shaves carefully, with a blade and a mug of hot lather.
...


They live and love in a motel room
With a small, happy dog...
They keep poems in boxes .... And read them daily
And decorate for holidays the best they can...

No shadows dance upon the sun
But the sun shines anyway
And their love has never dimmed....
And they believe art and life are one— no matter what you think....
                    —Samuel Hill, PhD


### A Jog-Trot Pair

Who were the twain that trod this track
So many times together
Hither and back,
In spells of certain and uncertain weather?

Commonplace in conduct they
Who wandered to and fro here
Day by day:
Two that few dwellers troubled themselves to know here.

The very gravel-path was prim
That daily they would follow:
Borders trim:
Never a wayward sprout, or hump, or hollow.

Trite usages in tamest style
Had tended to their plighting.
"It's just worthwhile,
Perhaps," they had said. "And saves much sad good-nighting."

And petty seemed the happenings
That ministered to their joyance:
Simple things,
Onerous to satiate souls, increased their buoyance.

Who could those common people be,
Of days the plainest, barest?
They were we;
Yes; happier than the cleverest, smartest, rarest.
                                        —Thomas Hardy

*Happiness*, not in another place but this place…
not for another hour, but this hour.
                                        —Walt Whitman

# About the Author

Jeffrey Ross, who resides in Arizona, is a writer, musician, and former full-time community college teacher. He has had four "Views" pieces published on *InsidehigherEd.com,* has authored and co-authored several national and international op-ed articles on community college identity, purpose, and culture, and has published numerous parody poems and articles. Ross co-authored the comic and critically acclaimed campus novel *College Leadership Crisis: The Philip Dolly Affair* (Rogue Phoenix Press, 2011). He also authored the romance parody *Love in the RV Park: A Romance for Men* (Rogue Phoenix Press, 2013), the nonfiction life history about 1920s life in Scottsdale, AZ *Silent Sonora* (Rogue Phoenix Press 2015), a mature romance *The Auroran: Cold Front Redemption* (Rogue Phoenix Press 2016), and the researched policy proposal *1040 Taxes Could be Replaced by One-Cent Fees!* (Rogue Phoenix Press 2018). Many readers have enjoyed his analysis of the community college experience, *At the Community College: Smiles and Reflections* (Rogue Phoenix Press, 2019). Ross, along with co-authors Brian Franzen and Michael Newlun, also wrote the interesting travel book *Southwest by Two Stroke: Riding 350 Yamahas to California*, which describes their 1973 motorcycle ride from Nebraska to California and back (Rogue Phoenix Press, 2019).

## Southwest by Two-Stroke

Our 1973 motorcycle ride took us from Beatrice, Nebraska, to Philmont Scout Ranch in New Mexico, Albuquerque, Phoenix, San Diego, LA, Vacaville, Lake Tahoe, Denver, and then back to Nebraska. We were teenagers, and we had relatives, friends, acquaintances, and girlfriends to see all along the journey. Some nights we camped out, others we stayed in a friend's travel trailer, and some nights we enjoyed regular beds and access to a swimming pool.

Each of us rode a 350cc two-stroke motorcycles on the 3500-mile trip. We had no cell phones, roadside assistance insurance coverage, custom ear plugs, or sound systems.

The early 70's was different than the 60's, but not that much different. The attraction of the open road and the Pacific Ocean was very powerful. None of us were worried about breaking down or the costs of the trip. We had to go see western America. And we did.

## At the Community College: Smiles and Reflections

Community colleges provide valuable learning experiences for millions of Americans. But they are not mini-universities or dedicated trade schools—they offer a unique higher-ed pathway which is often misunderstood and sometimes under-appreciated. This book provides a behind-the-scenes look at daily community college life—from student, administrative, board, and faculty perspectives! You will learn (or recognize) a great deal about daily community college machinations and the "characters" who are hard at work to make the community college journey "sustainable." Both humorous and revealing, the engaged reader will come away with a new appreciation for the American Community College Event!

## Silent Sonora

Silent Sonora details the life of a heroic young girl, Lillian Carroll, whose family resides in two tents during the 1920's and 1930's. Set in depression-era Scottsdale Arizona, this true story reveals Lillian's daily life experiences, the family's struggles, and her quest for a better life through education. Lillian tells readers directly about tent life, the local "emerging" Arizona communities, and the ongoing hardships she and her family confront. Both of Lillian's parents are deaf—her father works in the local agricultural industry, while her strong-willed mother endeavors to make the best home she can for her children. Lillian admits that "life was tough," but assures us she and her family had good times, too. Ultimately, Lillian's desire for a better education helps her situation—her love of family and strong faith give her the support she needs to finally gain independence.

## College Leadership Crisis: The Philip Dolly Affair

A Crisis in Community College Leadership: The Phillip Dolly Affair is literary in development but grounded in "chaotic" community college daily experience. The novel is comic, satiric, quasi-politically correct, edgy, and richly descriptive of community college life, leadership foibles, and cultural themes. This hyperbolic text is entertaining, edifying, and fun. Little community college fiction—comic or otherwise—exists—the authors are fearless in their humorous—and sometimes biting—analysis of community college culture....

The "stereotype-busting" authors reacquaint readers with the [faded] ideals of the 1960's social renaissance.

While community colleges are currently receiving heightened attention, this novel provides a behind-the-scenes analysis of many "whispered truths," those simmering but unspoken workplace issues, behaviors, and machinations nearly every worker [Everyman] in America will recognize.

## Love in the RV Park: A Romance for Men

This quirky and fast moving romance revolves around passionate lovers in tangled and mostly unfulfilling relationships. The tale is complete with hot housewives, rock musicians, exotic dancers, motorcycles, steamy nail polish-melting love scenes, hard drinking college professors, hybrid alien children, a romantic bug exterminator, girl fights, a New Year's Eve brawl, religious zealotry, prophecies (The Temple of Just DOET)—and more. Ultimately, Love in the RV Park is about the male perception (misperception?) of the female psyche—and the novel attempts to answer an age-old question: What do women want? Laugh or cry—you'll come away enlightened after reading this zany romance.

## The Auroran: Cold Front Redemption

August Nightingale, in late middle age, has had little success with relationships-- and not much meaningful satisfaction in the world of work. Abruptly deciding to "leave it all behind," he embarks on a snowy road trip to visit Civil War battlefields in Pennsylvania. His journey becomes one of self-realization. A mishap on the highway, the kindness of his beautiful neighbor Sarah (who helps him to convalesce), and the friendly people of Aurora change his life and his heart. This mature romance novel shows that it is never too late to find happiness, to experience meaningful love, when souls are honest and open to the truths of human experience.

## *1040 Taxes Could be Replaced by One-Cent Fees!*

1040 culture—like it or not—exists because the United States government taxes personal income to raise trillions to fund the federal treasury. This amount will undoubtedly increase in the future—but so will American commerce and the GDP. The focus of this book will be how we can raise 3.5 or 5.0 or 6 trillion dollars efficiently and accurately while eliminating the unwieldy 1040 tax return process. The TFP plan, basically, is to "automatically" assess a 1 cent fee (.01 dollar) on all trackable transactions in the US (or related international transactions using American financial institutions). Say good bye to tax preparation, deductions, refunds, credits—this will be a pay-as-you-go system. Tax audits and tax-related stress will become history.